Anonymous

Berea College, Kentucky

An interesting History - approved by the Prudential committee - 1883

Anonymous

Berea College, Kentucky
An interesting History - approved by the Prudential committee - 1883

ISBN/EAN: 9783337314361

Printed in Europe, USA, Canada, Australia, Japan

Cover: Foto ©Andreas Hilbeck / pixelio.de

More available books at **www.hansebooks.com**

BEREA COLLEGE,

KENTUCKY.

See Continuation inserted
at the end.

AN INTERESTING HISTORY,

APPROVED BY THE PRUDENTIAL COMMITTEE.

1883.

See continuation inserted
at the end.

CINCINNATI:
Elm Street Printing Company, Nos. 176 and 178 Elm Street.
1883.

BEREA COLLEGE.

———

B EREA is a village of about six hundred res-
ident inhabitants, situated in the southern
part of Madison County, one of the most popu-
lous and wealthy counties of the State of Kentucky. It is forty miles southeast from Lexington, and one hundred miles directly south from
Cincinnati, on the new extension of the Kentucky Central Railroad. From Louisville it is
about one hundred and thirty miles, by the
Knoxville branch of the Louisville and Nash-
ville Railroad. Two macadamized roads con-
nect it with the principal towns of the State.

Its name is borrowed from that place men-
tioned in the New Testament, whose inhabitants
were "more noble than those of Thessalonica,
because they searched the Scriptures daily."
The village contains about a dozen good houses
and ten stores, some of them quite small and
none of them spacious, and no liquor saloon or
grog shop.

IS IT WELL LOCATED?

Berea Ridge is about two miles long, of irregular shape, in some places narrow, in others wide or branching, and elevated about fifty feet above the surrounding country. The College grounds are near the center of this ridge, and on its widest part. Toward the south and east we look out upon a mountainous region, broken into more than a dozen distinct knobs from four hundred to eight hundred feet high, and from one mile to six miles distant. Each has its distinct name, and most of them are favorite resorts of companies seeking exercise and pleasure. To the north and west lie the rich, undulating blue grass lands, famous everywhere for their hemp, pastures, cattle, horses and magnificently formed men. These lands come within a mile of Berea, and spread out from sixty to eighty miles to the north and west.

The autumn scenery viewed from the observatory of the Ladies' Hall is exquisitely beautiful. The air is perfectly pure; every lot is easily drained; the water is soft and generally good, and is obtained by digging about fifteen feet. The climate is delightful, especially from April to December. There are, of course, stormy, windy days, and long, hot days in the summer;

but I have never experienced a day more oppressively hot here than in Chicago. The nights are always comfortable when the days are hottest. The soil is not rich, but, with proper culture, is very good for gardens and fruit.

But the location is well chosen for a more important reason. It is on the line of separation between two classes of people, as unlike each other in their physical development, their habits of life, and their views of society, as if they belonged to distinct races; and when we see them, on the morning of our Annual Commencement, pouring in by thousands—the rich in their carriages from the plains, and the poor from the mountains on horses and mules—and meeting on this common ground, we feel that the place was selected by Him who is "the Maker of them all." And when we look upon the crowd of three thousand people, white and colored, rich and poor, learned and ignorant, mingling without distinction and with perfect order, listening to speakers and singers of all shades of complexion, the words on the College seal seem wonderfully appropriate: "God hath made of one blood all nations of men." Twenty miles from this line, on either side, such a company could not be gathered.

ORIGIN OF THE COLLEGE—MR. FEE.

Rev. John G. Fee was born in Bracken County, Kentucky, in 1816. His father, a farmer, was a member of the Presbyterian Church, and the owner of thirteen slaves. John early embraced religion, and commenced preparation for the ministry. He entered college at Augusta, Kentucky, studied two years at Oxford, Ohio, and graduated at Augusta. His theological course was taken at Lane Seminary, Ohio, where, after much discussion, with earnest prayer for light, he became convinced of the great evil and sinfulness of American slavery. With a full sense of the obloquy and danger he must meet, he consecrated himself to preach the gospel of impartial love in his native State.

He first labored several months with his parents; but failing to persuade them to liberate their slaves, with great sadness he relinquished the effort, and carried the gospel to others. His father, a severe man, disowned and disinherited him, giving him one dollar in his will. His mother wept over her deluded son.

Before he became an abolitionist his father had given him a farm, in Indiana, which he sold for two thousand four hundred dollars, and spent the whole in buying and liberating a female slave, raised and married on the plantation, to prevent her being sold away; in publishing an antislavery manual; and in self-support. His people, in Lewis County, promised him one hundred dollars for preaching, but being offended by an antislavery sermon, very mild and gentle, paid him but twenty-five dollars. For two years he received two hundred dollars annually from the American Home Missionary Society; but finding that this society was aiding fifty-two slaveholding churches, he felt that he could not, conscientiously, solicit contributions for it, and hence must decline to receive its support.

On joining the Presbytery he made a full statement of his antislavery convictions. As these convictions ripened, his antislavery efforts multiplied. His church, in Lewis County, passed resolutions denouncing slavery as sinful, and refusing fellowship with slaveholders. The Synod reviewed this action, and censured Mr. Fee for disturbing the peace of Zion, and introducing a test of membership not known to the Constitution of the Presbyterian Church. Assured by the Presbytery that "repentance on their part was hopeless," after fully stating his views, he withdrew, and received a qualified letter of dismission. The publication of these facts in the

New York *Evangelist* brought him to the notice of the American Missionary Association, and its aid was offered him. From that time, for a period of thirty-four years, he received a large portion of his support from that society. He now declines further aid from this association; believing, as he does, that the association has departed from its former catholic work and is now doing a denominational work.

As formerly he was not willing to endorse slaveholding in any wise, so now he is not willing to endorse denominationalism in any wise.

In Lewis and Bracken Counties he labored eight years, and organized three antislavery churches. At the request of Cassius M. Clay he sent a box of the antislavery manuals, which were scattered through Madison County. The result was, the people invited him here, where, after preaching nine sermons, he organized a church which refused fellowship with slaveholders, and after one year he became its pastor. This relation he has now sustained twenty-eight years. There was little to encourage when he came. The place was a wilderness. It was inviting chiefly because it was central.

The same reasons which led to the organization of antislavery churches demanded an antislavery school. This was organized in 1855.

Its first teachers were Wm. E. Lincoln and Otis B. Waters, students of Oberlin College.

In 1856 Mr. Fee experienced a series of mobs in this region. He had before this been mobbed in Lewis, Mason and Bracken Counties. The first of this series was at Dripping Springs, in Garrard County; the next near Mt. Vernon, in Rock Castle County; the third, and most violent, was near Texas, in Madison County. Mr. Fee was preaching on the subject of Christian union, and was accompanied by Robert Jones, a native of the county, who was acting as a colporteur of the American Missionary Association. He was also encouraged by the two Messrs. Field and Marsh, residents in that vicinity. There was apprehension of danger, and Mr. Fee had been consulted as to the propriety of carrying guns. He said: "No; if I am disturbed I will appeal to the courts." He believed in the right of self-defense, but opposed the practice of carrying arms, and believed they were oftener a source of danger than a means of safety.

The sermon had commenced when a mob of sixty men, with pistols and guns, surrounded the house. One came in and said to Mr. Fee: "There are men here who wish you to stop and come out." He replied: "I am engaged in the exercise of a constitutional right and a religious duty; please do not interrupt," and preached on. The man went out and soon two others returned and demanded that he come out. He preached on. They seized him and dragged him out, no resistance being made. A man with a rope swore they would hang him to the first tree, unless he would promise to leave the county and never return. He replied: "I am in your hands. I would not harm you; if you harm me, the responsibility is with you. I can make no pledge; duty to God and my country forbid." They swore they would duck him in the Kentucky River as long as life was in him, unless he would promise to leave the county. He said: "I am a native of the State. I believe slavery is wrong. I am acting for the good of my country and all her people. You will know my motives at the judgment." He had proceeded but a few moments when one exclaimed: "We didn't come to hear a sermon; let us do our work." They stripped Robert Jones naked, bent him down, and gave him thirty-three lashes with three sycamore rods. He was so injured that he could not walk the next day. But he made no pledges and did not leave. They said to Mr. Fee: "We will give you five hundred lashes if you do not leave the county and promise never to return." He knelt down and said: "I will take my suffering; I can make no pledges." The whip was raised above him, but one cried: "Don't strike!" The man with the whip replied: "I feel that I ought to, but I don't like to go against my party. Get up and go home"—with an oath.

With Jones on his horse behind him, and ruffians in front and rear, he rode three miles, when the mob left him. They went into the woods, read the fourth chapter of Acts, and prayed. That night he preached in the house of Mr. Jones' cousin, and both the man and his wife covenanted to be the Lord's.

The church at Berea became terribly alarmed, and advised Mr. Fee to leave the State. For four weeks no man but Ham. Rawlings, a brave Kentuckian, entered his yard; none but women attended church. That brave man, Cassius M. Clay, though still friendly to Mr. Fee, notwithstanding their difference on the higher law question (Mr. Fee holding that a law confessedly contrary to the law of God ought not to be enforced), advised him to leave. But he continued his labors, Mr. Waters continued his school, and the excitement gradually died away. In the meantime two lawyers had been engaged to prosecute in behalf of Jones. The mob met in Richmond and swore they would give five hundred lashes to any lawyer who would prosecute the case.

The grand jury never inquired into it. Thirteen months after the mob, Prof. Rogers, the third teacher, closed a session of the school with ninety-six pupils and an exhibition, at which there were five hundred in attendance.

Four of the principal leaders of the mob soon came to violent deaths. So it was with all the mobs. Several of the most active in them soon died by violence. It became a common saying among them: "Old Master is against us."

PROF. ROGERS

Is a native of Cornwall, Connecticut. He prepared for college at Williams Academy, graduated at Oberlin, taught two or three years in New York City, and took his theological course at Oberlin. Being about to return West from a visit to New York, he was requested to take a company of orphans to Roseville, Illinois. He preached on Sunday, and on Monday was requested to remain. But he heard the call from Kentucky, and in 1858 came to the work in Berea, under the commission of the American Missionary Association, at a salary of four hundred dollars, walking eighty miles of the distance from Maysville. In a rude school-house, with a single unplastered room, without desks or the most common conveniences, he opened a sclect school with fifteen pupils. With an energy, enthusiasm, buoyancy, skill and love not wholly his own, he addressed himself to the work. Desks were supplied, maps and charts graced the walls, music and lectures were introduced. The young people were charmed; visitors from many miles away frequented the school, and before the close of the term a hundred names were enrolled. Mrs. Rogers, a charming little woman from Philadelphia, of Quaker parentage, leaving her babe during school hours with a nurse, went to the aid of her husband and added greatly to the enthusiasm.

The interest culminated in the exhibition at the close of the term. Teachers, pupils, and the whole community gave themselves heartily to preparation for the anticipated event. . The people, proud of their school, and the wonderful attainments of their children, and hopeful as to the future prosperity of their place, volunteered a public dinner to all who should attend. The exercises were held under a sylvan bower, constructed with exquisite taste. The pillars were grand old oaks, festooned with flowers. The light subdued by the thick matting of leaves and the joyous faces of a hundred pupils upon the extensive platform spread a charm over the whole audience, the largest ever assembled in the settlement; though "the glades" at the foot of the ridge had long been a place of public gatherings for horse races and political speeches. The hand of the Lord was manifestly in it. The closing speaker, a leading pupil, in reviewing the term and pronouncing his valedictory, was completely overcome with emotion, and for some moments the audience were in tears.

Brief, but enthusiastic speeches by gentlemen from a distance followed; and an ex-legislator from an adjoining county privately remarked: "If this school goes on, Kentucky is bound to become a free State; but I am going to hold on to my niggers as long as I can." After dinner a subscription was raised without difficulty to build an addition to the school-house, which still stands and is used for a district school.

The second term of the school was opened in September, and two additional teachers were employed, Mr. John G. Hanson and his wife, who brought to the work hearty enthusiasm, patient effort and full faith in the enterprise. A hundred pupils were gathered, not a few of them young men of fine abilities, some of whom have since exercised no small influence as teachers and professional men, and some have given their blood for their country. Though an antislavery spirit pervaded the school and the place, and the teachers expressed their sentiments with entire freedom and boldness, yet such was the reputation of the school and such the joyous atmosphere that pervaded it, that many young people from slaveholding families were attracted to it, and not a few became insensibly enamored with the love of liberty.

During this term, in the Young Men's Literary Society, the question was long and earnestly discussed, whether, if a colored person should apply for admission to the school, he should be rejected. This was the first public discussion of this question. It had previously been discussed and settled, as will appear, at a meeting held for the organization of a College Board of Trustees. Happily the question was not embarrassed by legal considerations, for there was no law of Kentucky forbidding education to free colored persons, or even to a slave, with his master's consent. As this was a question affecting the whole community, it became a topic of general interest. The opinion of all the teachers, as well as of him who was the father of the community, was decided and uniform, and may be expressed in a single declaration of the Principal of the school: "If any one made in God's image comes to get knowledge which will enable him to understand the revelation of God in Jesus Christ, he can not be rejected." This sentiment was not acceptable to the slaveholding families that patronized the school; and though none of the pupils left before the close of the term, the opposition became so great during the vacation, that few returned at the opening of the third term. But the school went on under the original teachers. Increased difficulties only inspired to greater efforts. The work they believed was of God and could not fail.

With the opening of the fourth term, in the fall of 1859, came additional encouragement. The affection of the former pupils had not ceased; the resolute perseverance, the manifest faith and cheerful hope of those, who, according to ordinary calculations, should have been discouraged, impressed the people that perhaps a Divine power was sustaining them, and they might succeed. But before the close of the term an event occurred in Virginia which shook the very foundations of the school, though it did not destroy them. Before describing the effects of the John Brown raid, as felt in Berea, we will return and take up a thread that was dropped.

THE COLLEGE CHARTER AND CONSTITUTION.

The first effort made to form a constitution for the College, of which Berea School was the embryo, was made on the seventh of September, 1858, when several gentlemen met for that purpose at Mr. Fee's residence, and appointed him Chairman of the meeting; J. G. Hanson, Secretary; and Mr. Rogers Chairman of a Committee to draw up the proposed constitution. At that meeting a constitution was reported, discussed and agreed upon, and signed by those present. In order to secure the co-operation of gentlemen who could not be present, the meeting adjourned to meet in December. The meeting was held, and several subsequent meetings, but it was not till the following July that the present constitution, essentially the same as the first, was adopted. At this meeting, after much prayer, three topics of inquiry were considered. First: "Is there a demand for a permanent College of such a character as we have in view here?" Secondly: "Are we the men called of God to carry it forward?" Thirdly: "Is it to be for God, and for him alone?" By the third topic of inquiry it was the desire of those making it to examine themselves and see if, so far as their knowledge extended, they could

2

give up all selfish motives in going forward with the work. Undoubtedly, however honest they were, Infinite Wisdom saw in their hearts that which, when developed, would call for great humiliation on their part and mercy on His; but He who accepts the earnest desire to do His will, did not despise their weakness or ignorance of themselves, of which they have had occasion since then to learn not a little.

After days of discussion upon various points, almost all of them pertaining to the Christian character of the school, a constitution and by-laws were adopted. Two of the by-laws will sufficiently indicate the wishes of those who were planning for the future of the Institution:

"This College shall be under an influence strictly Christian, and, as such, opposed to sectarianism, slaveholding, caste, and every other wrong institution or practice."

"The object of this College shall be to furnish the facilities for a thorough education to all persons of good moral character, at the least possible expense to the same, and all the inducements and facilities for manual labor which can reasonably be supplied by the Board of Trustees shall be offered to its students."

This constitution was signed by Rev. John G. Fee, Rev. J. S. Davis, Rev. Geo. Candee, John

Smith, Wm. Stapp, T. J. Renfro, John G. Hanson and Rev. J. A. R. Rogers; and four other gentlemen were invited to unite with them in taking steps to obtain a charter under a general law of the State. Many difficulties arose in obtaining suitable co-operation and completing the preliminary steps for obtaining a charter. Meanwhile a tract of land, which was felt to be the most desirable for the College ground, was offered for sale. Four of the Trustees, on their own responsibility, purchased the tract, containing more than a hundred acres, for one thousand eight hundred dollars, and Mr. Fee was asked to go East to obtain funds for securing the same for the College. It was while he was absent that the John Brown raid occurred, which had so potent an influence upon the future of the Berea School.

Before this raid, as has been already stated, Berea had become an object of suspicion and hatred. Any influence for liberty was regarded with great jealousy, and coming in the form of a school giving promise of becoming important, it was generally felt that it must be put down. Yet in Kentucky there was enough of the old traditional love of free speech and fair play to prevent any acts of violence against an Institution intrenched in the hearts of many, and with which no fault could be found, save that it was exerting an influence in favor of freedom.

But when John Brown made his raid, it was felt by some that an opportunity had arisen for the suppression of the school. All Northern men were regarded as dangerous, and especially those who openly and fearlessly opposed slavery. Who knew but that John Brown's band was only one of a hundred others scattered through the South for the purpose of stirring up insurrection among the slaves? It was urged that there were many strong, if not decisive, proofs that the colony at Berea was one whose ultimate aim was violence. A number of families were moving into Berea, and some had left their families behind. Then what should bring them to such a place as Berea, where the soil was regarded as too poor to enable men to get a comfortable living, but some sinister motive? Again the location of Berea, at the base of the foothills of the Cumberland Mountains, was perfect in a strategic point of view, and it was by no means certain that the Bereans could not exercise a controlling influence over the mountain men. By reason of such declarations, and abundant false rumors, and the real fear produced throughout the South by the John Brown raid, many were really alarmed. Women told their husbands that they could not sleep at night, and that the Bereans must be driven out of the State. It was announced in one of the papers that a box of Sharpe's rifles had been intercepted on the way to Berea. In view of this fact it was thought prudent by some gentlemen in Richmond to examine several heavy boxes containing the household goods of Rev. John Boughton, who had moved to Berea. Accordingly, at night, they carefully examined some of the most suspicious-looking boxes in one of the warehouses. At first all seemed to be right, and the boxes to contain nothing but the usual family goods; finally, however, some trepidation may have been produced by the discovery of what was declared to be an "infernal machine," which turned out to be a large set of Yankee candle-molds. In consequence of this state of things, several organized efforts were made to suppress the school, and drive those who were directing it out of the State. The first and second efforts for uniting the people of Madison County as a whole for this despicable work proved abortive. At length a new wave of terror having swept over the State, and the people having become more intensely excited by virulent and false statements in the newspapers of the county and other parts of the State, a mass meeting was held at the Court House in Richmond, violent speeches were made, and a committee of sixty-five, composed of the wealthiest and "most respectable" citizens of the county, was appointed, to secure the removal from the State, peacefully if possible, within ten days, of Rev. John G. Fee and Rev. J. A. R. Rogers, and such others as the committee should think necessary for the public quiet and safety. A long address to the people of the county and community at large was adopted by the meeting. In this address it was set forth that liberty and slavery could not dwell together, that in a slave State men advocating liberty were a dangerous element, and that, as self-preservation was the first law of nations as well as individuals, and that, as it was a settled matter that Kentucky was to remain a slave State, it was essential to the peace of the commonwealth that the school at Berea should be suppressed, and those who were its originators and supporters should be driven from the State; and that, although this could not be done by law, necessity was higher than all law. It was the old doctrine of Caiaphas, truer than he knew, that the few must suffer for the good of the many. Assuming that it was right and just that Kentucky should be perpetually a slave State, the argument would have some force.

Meanwhile the people of Berèa were having additional experiences in their life of trial. The air was dark with threats. It did not sound pleasantly in the ears of a delicate woman to be told that her husband was to be hung to a limb before the school-room door. The Principal of the school wrote to the press denying the assertions in regard to the Bercans, and correcting the false report of Mr. Fee's speech in Brooklyn, but could not get a hearing. So abundant were the threats against Mr. Fee that he was advised not to return to the State. With characteristic courage he determined to come, but was providentially hindered by an accident in Cincinnati. The people of Berea gathered together every night to pray for God's protection and guidance, and most marvelously were the Scriptures opened to their understanding. They could now easily see why Luther felt that he could not have lived but for the Hundred and eighteenth Psalm. The Thirty-seventh Psalm seemed written especially for them, and not only calmed their fears but cheered their hearts.

At length, after several days of expectation, the mob, the "organized gentlemen," appeared. On the twenty-third of December, 1859, while Mr. Rogers' family were at dinner in the cottage which he had just erected in the woods adjoin-

ing the grounds selected for the College, and not
yet surrounded by a fence, it was hastily announced that the men had come. He stepped
to the front door, and there sixty horsemen,
more or less, completely armed, were forming
themselves in wedge shape before the house. He
stepped out of the door, and at once the leader
of the band came up and delivered to him a document, demanding in the name of the committee
that he should leave the county within ten days.
He attempted to reason with the leader, and told
him that if he had violated any law of the State,
he was willing to abide the consequences, that
he was quietly laboring for the good of the community and the support of his family, and that
in the exercise of his rights he must not be disturbed.   A disturbance arose in the crowd, and
the whole company then wheeled and went to
ten other families, most of them native Kentuckians, and left a similar document.   Everything was done in as orderly and unobjectionable
a manner as possible.

Those warned to leave the State, and others
most interested, met for prayer and deliberation.
Some thought that when persecuted in one city
it was duty to flee to another, and that it was
plainly the part of wisdom for those who must
cope with the mass of the people if they re-

mained, to go quietly away.   Others counseled to remain till forcibly removed.   No decision was reached.   On the following day it was decided to appeal to the Governor of the State for protection, though with scarcely a ray of hope that it would be of any avail.   The following petition was adopted:

To His Excellency, the Governor of the State of Kentucky:

We, the undersigned, loyal citizens and residents of the State of Kentucky and County of Madison, do respectfully call your attention to the following facts:

1. We have come from various parts of this and adjoining States to this county, with the intention of making it our home, have supported ourselves and families by honest industry, and endeavored to promote the interests of religion and education.

2. It is a principle with us to "submit to every ordinance of man for the Lord's sake, unto governors as unto them that are sent by him for the punishment of evil-doers and the praise of them that do well," and in accordance with this principle we have been obedient in all respects to the laws of this State.

3. Within a few weeks evil and false reports have been put into circulation, imputing to us motives, words and conduct calculated to inflame the public mind, which imputations are utterly false and groundless.   These imputations we have publicly denied, and offered every facility for the fullest investigation, which we have earnestly but vainly sought.

3

4. On Friday, the twenty-third inst., a company of sixty-two men, claiming to have been appointed by a meeting of the citizens of our county, without any shadow of legal authority, and in violation of the constitution and laws of the State and United States, called at our respective residences and places of business, and notified us to leave the county and State, and be without this county and State within ten days, and handed us the accompanying document, in which you will see that unless the said order be promptly complied with, there is expressed a fixed determination to remove us by force.

In view of these facts, which we can substantiate by the fullest evidence, we respectfully pray that you, in the exercise of the power vested in you by the constitution, and made your duty to use, do protect us in our rights as loyal citizens of the State of Kentucky.

J. A. R. ROGERS,   SWINGLEHURST LIFE,

J. G. HANSON,   JOHN SMITH,

I. D. REED,   E. T. HAYES,

JAS. S. DAVIS,   CHAS. E. GRIFFIN,

JOHN F. BOUGHTON, A. G. W. PARKER,

W. H. TORRY.

BEREA, MADISON CO., KY., *December* 24, 1859.

The petition was taken by two of their number to Governor Magoffin, who received them courteously, but replied that the public mind was deeply moved by the events in Virginia, and that he could not engage to protect them from their fellow-citizens, who had resolved that they must go.

At last it became plain to all that they must leave the State for the present, but with the sure expectation of returning again in due time. So confident were some of them made, by the Spirit of God, in regard to their return, that they doubted it scarcely more than the rising of the morrow's sun. They believed in God and his righteousness, and his love of the poor and oppressed, and clearly foresaw that such conduct would only hasten the day of freedom. They plainly declared to friends and foes that they were going away, but that they should return again. They had no disposition to sell their homes. They counted them worth not a dollar less than before the troubles in Virginia. Sore were the partings between those who left and those who remained.

The whole community gathered as the exiles left, and under the broad sky, with bared heads and trusting hearts, they were committed to the care of Almighty God by Rev. George Candee, who had come from his home in Jackson County to cheer with his undaunted faith those who were about to leave. The ten families which left numbered about forty persons, and were mercifully guided by the God of all grace and wisdom.

They went in various directions, and engaged in such work as came to hand, making no per-

manent engagements, but waiting the call of
God to return to their former homes. Soon the
war broke out, and the exiles plainly saw that,
if they had been permitted to remain in Berea,
the school must have been suspended.

Mr. Fee met his retiring friends in Cincinnati
and fully approved their course, but was not yet
convinced of the necessity of his leaving his native
State. He went over to Bracken County to ful-
fill an appointment, though Mr. Mallet, a teacher
from Oberlin, had recently been mobbed there,
and Mr. Davis, a preacher, also from Oberlin,
had been mobbed in Lewis County. A county
meeting was called, about eight hundred attended,
and a committee of sixty-two warned him and
others to leave. He made no promises but to do
what should seem to be duty. All friends advised him to leave the State. A day of fasting
and prayer was observed. His decision was that
he had no right seriously to imperil his friends
against their will, and he left.

After some months he brought the corpse of
his little boy to the cemetery of the Free Church
of Christ in Bracken. Immediately he became
deeply impressed with the conviction that he
ought to return to his native State, and there
preach the gospel of impartial love; and knowing something of the obloquy and peril of then

attempting such a work, after a severe mental
struggle he entered into covenant with God to
return and thus labor. He came with grave-
stones for the little mound, and a mob took him
from the omnibus; but they soon released him,
and he preached the next Sabbath.

One of the prominent Trustees of Berea College, and for a short time a teacher, was

JOHN G. HANSON,

A native of Bracken County, Kentucky. About
the first of March, 1860, he returned to Berea
for the purpose of sawing some three hundred
logs left at his mill, and of selling the mill, unless he found the way open for his remaining.
The next Monday being county-court day, the
Mob Committee convened and agreed to meet
at the Glade Meeting House on Saturday, for
the removal of Mr. Hanson. Only thirty-five
met, and with a few speeches and much whisky
they dispersed, two of them going to the mill
and carrying off an iron eagle, an ornament on
the mill, which was returned to its place the
next day. It was then thought the mob spirit
had nearly died out. But as events proved it
was passing from the original "sixty-five sensible and discreet men" to those sunk so low in
vice and pollution as to seem "condemned

already." Even C. M. Clay advised Mr. Hanson's friends not to stand by him. Monday
morning twenty-five armed men searched his
boarding-place, and swore they would search
every house in the neighborhood, but they would
have him and he "should hang." But he had
escaped to the woods without being seen, and at
night he traveled twenty miles afoot into Jackson County, where for a week he hid in cliffs
and caves in the daytime, and at night went to
a friend's house for food and lodging. The mob
went from house to house, threatening to shoot
people unless they would tell them where Mr.
Hanson was. As they approached the house of
George West, his daughter, a young woman,
fastened the door, and they broke it down upon
her and walked over it while she lay under it.
They rushed to her father, who sat up in his
bed propped up with pillows, being low with
consumption, and, putting their pistols to his
breast, demanded where Hanson was. In the
meantime the daughter, a motherless orphan, had
extricated herself from the door, and one of the
ruffians thrust his pistol against her breast and
pressed her back against a cupboard, cursing her
for shutting the door against them. Vile language was addressed to a younger sister. In
Rock Castle County they broke down the door

of Mr. Burdett's house, and, putting their pistols to the breasts of his wife and daughters,
threatened to shoot if they did not reveal the
hiding-place of Mr. Hanson.   This they re-
peated again and again; but as he could nowhere
be found, they returned to Berea.   On their way
they met a company of Berea men going to Mr.
West's, having heard of his ill treatment.   Both
parties cried out: "Don't shoot!"   The mob fired
about thirty shots, by the order of Colonel
Mundy, and the Berea men returned two.   None
were seriously injured.   Having accomplished
nothing they returned to Richmond for recruits.
A cannon was secured from Lexington, and the
next day they returned to Berea, two hundred
and nineteen strong.   Finding no Berea men at
home they went to Mr. Hanson's mill, tore off
the roof, pulled down the smoke stack, broke
every wheel, ruined the boiler, and left all a
complete wreck.   They unroofed a neighbor's
smoke house, tore a log from the wall of his
dwelling, pulled his chimney down and shot
many of his chickens.   Then, leaving the names
of fifteen men, who they said must leave in fifteen days, they returned to Richmond, and, as
an eye-witness asserts, the circuit court adjourned
to hear their report.   Such a state of society had
slavery produced.

Many in Jackson County urged Mr. Hanson to remain with them, and pledged their lives, their property and their sacred honor in defense of his rights. But not willing to bring on a conflict between the two counties, and knowing that his life was in constant danger, he determined to leave the State. On the third of April he left the mountain fastnesses, and, walking all that night, he passed his beloved home and his mill in ruins. The next day, having passed the small town of Kirksville, he was pursued by two of the original committee of "sixty-five sensible and discreet men." They searched him for "fighting tools," as they said; but he assured them he never carried any, and had no wish to hurt any man, and was then going out of the State. They told him they were in honor bound to deliver him in Richmond. A brother of one of the committee told him he must now go to Richmond and "pull rope." And they started slowly on, the committee riding and he walking in front. But they knew that to take him to Richmond was to murder him, and they began to shrink from such a crime. One proposed to let him go, and got off his horse and requested him to ride. Finally, after a long consultation, they told him that they had been deceived in him, that they did not wish to see a hair of his head hurt, that a reward of

one hundred dollars was offered for his delivery
in Richmond, but they would not deliver him.
They advised him to endeavor to escape, and
gave him directions for his safety. Leaving
them he crossed Kentucky River, on his way to
the Kentucky Central Railroad at Nicholasville.
He found he was pursued and lay in the fields
all night, and barely escaped being retaken. He
desired to find some "Charter Oak" in which to
conceal the archives of the young Institution,
which he bore with him, being still its Secretary,
as he continued to be fourteen years. He spent
the most of the night and the next day on the
Cedar Bluffs of Hickman Creek, near where
Camp Nelson was afterward located. The next
night he passed Nicholasville, at early dawn
passed between Lexington and Ashland, and
reached Paris in time for the cars, which he took
to Falmouth. Thence he walked nine miles, and
slept in a house the first time for a week. A
weary walk of fourteen miles brought him to his
father's house, thankful for God's protection and
for warm and true hearts to cheer him.

Mr. Hanson closes his narrative, of which this
is an abstract, with the following expression of
his feelings:

"When I reflect what my course of life and
my labors have been, what I had at heart and

wished to do for my countrymen in Kentucky,
and think of what I have received at their hands,
it makes me weep and love them more; as they
show by their madness that 'they know not what
they do,' and are tending fast to eternal sorrows.
In the course that I have followed I have nothing that I regret. Trusting in God I shall still
labor that so good a land, filled with many generous spirits, and many wailing slaves, shall yet
be free."

Mr. Hanson returned at the close of the war,
and found that justice, which had "stood afar
off," was coming nigh. He recovered a portion
of his loss, rebuilt his shattered mill, and, with
the aid of his brother, erected another, and also
a planing mill. But not one-fourth the damage
done him has been made good. He is still a
Trustee of the College and a member of the
Prudential Committee.

In 1862 Mr. Fee made another effort to return
to the State. He sent his family forward to
Berea, but in attempting to join them was
stopped by the battle of Richmond, and for ten
weeks no communication passed between them.

That year he was mobbed in Augusta, where
he graduated. He was taken into the office of
his cousin, and, after being threatened with death
if he should ever return, was put across the Ohio

River at midnight. Two skiff loads of ruffians
followed, swearing that they would whip him
like hell; but on landing in the darkness they
failed to find him. Four of the leaders of this
mob died sudden and violent deaths.

Five weeks later he returned to Bracken
County, and was mobbed while waiting for the
stage at the house of a Presbyterian minister in
an adjoining county. He was committed to five
men to be taken to Augusta. But a friend
joined the company and adroitly diverted them
to Maysville, where he crossed the river. Being
assured by friends that he could not travel in
Kentucky, he turned aside to a village in Ohio,
sent for his family and remained some ten
months, then returned to Berea, where his wife,
aided by his oldest son, opened a school.

Till the close of the war much of his time was
spent in Camp Nelson, a natural fortress, with
sublime scenery and a rich soil, almost encircled
by the high and rugged banks of the Kentucky
River, nineteen miles south of Lexington and
thirty-six from Berea. Here he aided in establishing schools for colored soldiers and their
women and children, and here had a little of his
peculiar experience. Among seven white teachers a single bright, genteel quadroon was introduced, and five of the seven refused to eat with

her. He was advised to remove her, but refused. The average Kentuckian would say: "The five did just right." Bereans would say: "They did just wrong." At Camp Nelson there is still a large colored settlement—moral, harmonious and hopeful. The school still continues, and is at present under the supervision of a Board of Trustees.

This brief account of the persecutions and hardships of those days of trial needs to be filled up by the reader's imagination; and there is little danger that the matter will be overdone. The thrilling stories of our sisters, with which, hour after hour, they enchain the wives of us who were not actors in those scenes, would form an interesting chapter of annoyances, and dangers, and marvelous deliverances, of midnight watchings, and fears, and prayers, of cheerful courage, and faith, and hopes delayed, of the self-sacrificing adherence and protection of some, and the contemptuous scorn and perfidy of others, which it would be easy to write; but our object is not a story, but a plain, historical account of Berea College.

REOPENING OF THE SCHOOL.

In 1865 the school was reopened. Prof. Rogers and family returned, and W. W. Wheeler and wife came from Camp Nelson, as assistants.

A charter for a College was obtained under a general law of the State, the Board of Trustees was reorganized, other lands were purchased, students came in to the number of seventy-five or more, and everything seemed promising; when a new question arose, or rather an old question in a practical form. Before the war, when it was decided to "furnish facilities for education to all persons of good moral character," three of the Trustees had resigned; for *all* persons included colored persons—and the discussion of the question, whether, if a colored person should ask for admission to the school, he should be rejected, had greatly diminished the number of pupils. Now the question took a practical shape. Three colored youths asked admission. This raised no difficult question. But one decision was possible to such men; and that was already made. They were "persons of good moral character," and must be admitted. But it was manifest that a tempest of opposition would follow, mobs might rally again, and the school might be broken up. Though duty was plain, the consequence might be like a crucifixion. The morning that those three harmless youths walked in, half the school walked out. The whole country was excited, and, but for the discipline of the war, and the awe produced by the triumph of liberty over slavery, and the abolitionists of Berea over their enemies, doubtless another expulsion would have been chronicled. Rumors of raids came from far, and rowdyism sometimes disgraced itself very near. Pistols were discharged by drunken rowdies racing through the streets, and occasionally were fired into the buildings. But the opposition generally confined itself to exhibitions of disgust, and such published declarations as " Berea is a stench in the nostrils of all true Kentuckians"—delicate words once published by a State Superintendent of Public Schools and by our own country paper. But this we could well endure, so long as we knew of but one school more patronized by Kentuckians than this. This year our two county papers published very fair and complimentary accounts of our commencement. The vacancy made by the white deserters was soon filled with colored recruits, and eventually nearly all that left returned and became fast friends of Berea. At no time have the colored exceeded two-thirds of the school, and one year there were two more white than colored. The evils which wise ones knew would result from this union have never appeared. The most serious collision which the writer remembers to have occurred between the races was where an uncultured white girl complained

that a colored girl called her "poor white trash,"
and the colored girl replied that she did not do
it till she called her "nigger." The controversy
was settled without great difficulty. There is no
school in the State easier governed than this.
The question whether the colored pupils are not
necessarily a drag upon the classes would never
be asked by one who had any fair criterion by
which to judge. Pupils who have had the best
school advantages from their infancy, *ceteris
paribus*, will surpass those who learn their al-
phabet at fifteen or eighteen. This is the chief
source of inequality among our students. The
certain amalgamation which was to follow is all
in the future. What dangers await us in this
respect we know not; but of this we feel sure,
that any alliances which may possibly result
from the social relations established here will be
a blessing compared with the disgusting concubi-
nage which abounded in the days of slavery, and
is so very common still. We feel sure also that
freedom, education and equality will tend, not
to promote, but to cure all social evils. All history proves that the beautiful women in the
lower walks of life are a prey to lustful men who
look down upon them from a more elevated position. Aside from pure religion we know of no
so sure protection for them as social elevation,

which carries with it self-respect and commands the respect of others. But all such reasoning aside, we know it can not be dangerous to love our neighbors as ourselves, and do to others as we would that they should do to us. The influence which has kept the colored population in a degraded condition, and still seeks to keep them there, is not love and justice, but lust and oppression. For more than fifty years some of us have heard this amalgamation alarm, but it seldom came from those who "remembered them that were in bonds as bound with them;" but was always loudest, as it still is, from those who have the least care what becomes of either white or colored people, so that their own selfish lives are not interrupted.

We know that many good people have their honest fears on this subject, and we shall always be thankful for their advice and prayers in discharging our most difficult and delicate responsibilities.

Many of our friends desire to know precisely what relations our white and colored pupils sustain to each other, and it is our desire that they should know.

Our school regulations make no distinction whatever on account of color. They recite in the same classes, eat at the same tables, room in the same buildings, attend the same meetings and meet in all general social gatherings. It is no uncommon thing on such occasions as Thanksgiving and Christmas to see three hundred persons—teachers, pupils and citizens—mingling in the most friendly relations, without the least friction or the least sense of impropriety. Do persons of different races and sexes attend each other to and from literary lectures and social assemblies? There is no rule against it, and sometimes they do. If we saw that the parties were in danger of exposing themselves to violence, or special suspicion of improper motives, or were disposed to make an offensive display of themselves, we should interfere to prevent it. If such parties should become especially intimate, and appear to be contemplating a life union, being, as teachers, to a great extent, in *loco parentis*, we should remind them of the contempt and ostracism society would visit upon them, and if thought necessary communicate with their parents. But even such an alliance, if conducted in other respects with propriety and discretion, would not disturb their relations to the school. Their own judgment and the social influences bearing upon them are their best and only necessary protection against an imprudent decision.

We are often asked how our white pupils en-

4

dure this condition of things. They come with
a perfect knowledge of the character of the
school, and with their minds prepared to endure
it; and, having remained a week or two, they
find there is nothing to endure. The difference
between a colored person's sitting at the table
and standing by it is too slight to be disturbed
about; and the difference between lifting at the
same log and working at the same problem is
hardly discoverable. They never did shrink
from contiguity with colored people and why
should they now? The trouble is at the other
end of the line and not here. A prominent gen-
tleman, a democrat and ex-rebel, a preacher and
distinguished educator, living sixty miles distant,
met one of our professors at a Sabbath-School
convention, and the President at a teachers' institute, a white student at another institute, and
a colored student as a teacher in his county, and
became convinced that Berea College was the
best school for his own son. With a great struggle, himself, and wife, and son overcame their
own prejudices, and concluded to bear the contempt of their neighbors. The father informed
a democratic, Christian brother that he had concluded to send his son to Berea, and he at once
replied: "You had better take him out and shoot
him!" On their way here they avoided the

houses of old friends to escape unpleasant talk.
Their trouble was not here. Many of their
neighbors have also availed themselves of the
same advantages, and the trouble is greatly diminished there.

Four nice young ladies came one hundred and
twenty miles to attend the school, but said they
were obliged to fight their way here and that we
had no idea what opposition they had to contend
with. One of them received a letter from a
young friend informing her that if she came
home at the close of the first term she would
probably be received into society again, but she
could never occupy the place she formerly did.
She thanked him for his interest in her welfare,
and assured him that her true friends would not
forsake her, and told him that probably some of
her friends needed to be tried. Another was
told that she must not expect to be employed as
a teacher in that country; but she soon obtained
one of the best schools, and all felt so little dam-
aged that they were very anxious to return.

A lady came here to reside for the sake of educating her son, but not till her friends had secured a promise that the daughter should never
attend the school. What compromise has been
made I am not aware, but the daughter is now
attending and enjoys it very much. It is a moral

discipline for a white Kentuckian to attend Berea
College, which is often more valuable than the
mere scientific knowledge obtained.

We are often advised by our Kentucky visitors that a single change would add greatly to
the usefulness and prosperity of our school. If
we would just separate the blacks by themselves,
and instruct them as we do now, only in separate buildings, we would be crowded with students and money would flow in upon us abun-
dantly. It seems as if we were standing in our
own light. We reply that this would double
the expenses of the school, and the two departments might as well be in different towns; also
it would defeat one of the chief objects of the
school, to eradicate prejudice and caste; also we
ask what other school in the State has been enabled by its friends to furnish as good buildings
and as good an education as we, at as low a rate?
Also we inform them that money enough could
not be offered to induce us to make such a
change.

On the general question of admitting persons
of good moral character, without regard to race
or color, the school has maintained a uniform
position; but as to the application of the general
principle, in particular cases, difficult questions
have arisen and considerable diversity of views

has existed. It is not without much discussion, and serious misgivings on the part of some, that we have reached all the practical principles here explained in detail. So far as appears there is perfect harmony among us at present, and for ten years there has been no discussion on these subjects.

TEMPORARY BUILDINGS.

A large influx of students in 1866-7 necessitated the furnishing of room. Two buildings, suitable for stores, were erected. One was used for a boarding hall, the upper story and the attic being divided into rooms for young ladies and lady teachers, and the other for a store and dwelling.

Two nice, but cheap, little cottages were erected for dormitories for young men, and three box houses, about fifteen by thirty, of rough plank, with outside stairways to the attics for the same purpose. Another building of similar construction, thirty-two by sixty-four, was divided into three school-rooms, a hall and a chapel. The whole building was soon needed as a chapel. It was whitewashed and tolerably comfortable in the summer, but cold in the winter.

These buildings, from top to bottom, were filled with students, some occupying attics where

they could hardly stand erect, when President
E. H. Fairchild came, in the spring of 1869. He
was called at the meeting of the trustees in July,
1868.

PRESIDENT FAIRCHILD.

He is a native of Stockbridge, Massachusetts,
but was reared in Northern Ohio. He and his
brother James, now President of Oberlin College, constituted the first Freshman Class of that
institution. Their father was a farmer of moderate means, yet was able, with great economy,
and the hearty co-operation of all the family, to
send three sons and two daughters through the
entire college course at Oberlin; and another
daughter through the ladies' course, and the
sons through the theological department. Ed-
ward Henry, the President of Berea College, at
the early age of sixteen, while a student at the
Elyria High School, under the supervision of
John Monteith, became greatly interested in the
antislavery movement, which was beginning to
stir the hearts of a few in many parts of the
country. At the close of six months' discussion
of the subject in the school, he, with a school-
mate, prepared a colloquy for the public exhibition held in the Court House, in which they
represented a slave trader, a planter, a driver, a
slave pen in hearing, but not in sight, its keeper,

an abolitionist, a slave sold, whipped and libera-
ted, with hot blood and high words, and a show
of weapons. The whole county was excited by
it. At Oberlin he participated in the long and
earnest discussion of the question of admitting
colored students. He was present when the pro-
testing students from Lane, with President Ma-
han and Prof. Morgan, were welcomed, and
listened to the twenty-one lectures of Theodore
Weld, delivered soon after. At twenty-one,
when good material was not abundant, he was
commissioned as an antislavery lecturer by the
American Antislavery Society, and sent three
months to Northern Pennsylvania. At twenty-
two he was engaged for four months, as teacher
of a large colored school at the foot of Western
Row in Cincinnati, receiving his expenses for
his salary. At twenty-three he was employed
three months by the Ohio Anti-slavery Society.
In these various labors for the oppressed he received his share of attention from mobs, and
cold shoulder from preachers; and once, at
Columbus in Pennsylvania, after speaking an
hour amid a din of horns, tin pans, swearing,
screeching, singing, and flying missiles, was driven
from the house by burning brimstone. At twen-
ty-six, having finished his theological studies,
and taken for his companion the maid whom his

heart selected when he was fifteen, he was called
to preach to the First Congregational Church of
Cleveland. Having continued in the ministry
twelve years, in various places, he was appointed
Principal of the Preparatory Department of Oberlin Collge, and held that position sixteen years,
having supervision of five hundred young men
and over forty teachers each year. The last two
years he acted as financial agent of the college
and raised eighty thousand dollars. This work
called the attention of incipient institutions to
him, and, while desired at Oberlin, he received
three appointments, almost simultaneously, from
three colleges, remote from each other, all of
them desirable, and a visit from a fourth. He
accepted the call to Berea, after a visit to the
place, and entered upon the work in April, 1869.
This year Howard Hall was erected by the
Freedmen's Bureau, at a cost of eighteen thousand dollars. It is a very fine three-story wood
building, forty by eighty, with a tin roof, and
presents a much better appearance than its pic-
ture.

It is a dormitory for young men, and embraces
a reading room and two society rooms now oc-
cupied by students.

HOWARD HALL.

LADIES' HALL.

In 1870–71 our accommodations for young ladies were found much too strait for them. Nine were sent into the attic, which was one large room, with a window in each end. There was no room for further development, and such accommodations as we had were of a very inferior style. The dining room was also used for common sitting room and parlor. A new building was a necessity; but whether to erect a temporary or a permanent edifice was an important question. After consulting friends on whom we must largely depend for the means, it was determined to erect such a building as would meet our wants for many years, not with the expectation of filling it immediately, but, as we hoped, in a few years. The Ladies' Hall at Oberlin was taken as a pattern, and its excellencies were, if possible, improved, and its defects remedied. It is one of the most perfect buildings of its kind to be found in the country. It is of brick, three stories high, above a superior basement, having two fronts of one hundred and twenty feet each, and a roof of slate and tin. The first story embraces a reception room, office, parlor, assembly room, society room, reading room, dressing room, a large dining room, an upper kitchen with a china closet and variety room, and the steward's

5

rooms. The basement, which on one side is entirely above ground, embraces, besides furnaces and wood rooms and cellar rooms, a superb kitchen, with a meal room and the cook's living room adjoining, and dumb waiters, a porter's room contiguous to the elevator and the furnaces, a wash room and ironing room, and a railroad for carrying trunks to the elevator and wood to every place where it is needed. The two upper stories furnish rooms for ninety ladies, with water tanks, water closets and bath rooms on both floors. The first story and the corridors are heated by three superior furnaces, and the rooms in the two upper stories with stoves. Every room has a ventilator and a transom, and every lady's room a closet. The whole is finished with butternut and chestnut, and varnished. The garret is one large room, with a smooth, nice floor over the whole, an excellent place for exercise or for drying clothes in stormy weather. A door from the wash room opens to the elevator. Besides the tanks in the building, there are three large cisterns and a large well outside. There is also a forcing pump to send water from the well, which never fails, to the tanks above. This building is surrounded with six acres of ground, embracing a large grove of forest trees at one side, coming up to the street, in which,

CHAPEL.

by permission, young gentlemen may meet the
ladies for croquet. In the rear of this grove is
a vineyard, and in the rear of the vineyard a
garden. The front yard is graded and covered
with grass, dotted with evergreens, and furnished
with permanent walks of slate and gravel. On
the two fronts is a beautiful and substantial
picket fence. The cost of the whole, including
the ground and a substantial barn, was fifty
thousand dollars.

All other college buildings, including Howard
Hall, Recitation Hall, which is a transformation
of the second boarding hall, Office Building,
Grammar School, Intermediate School, Primary
School, very good buildings, and the Chapel, a
very fine building costing $9,000, lighted with
gas, are situated in the College Campus, consist-
ing of two large and beautiful groves of forest
trees, embracing about forty-five acres. The
larger grove, in which the buildings are, is on
the high land, and the other in the plain, fifty
feet below.

FINANCE.

Besides the buildings, which are estimated at
eighty-two thousand dollars, the College owns
three hundred acres of land, not including the
grounds about the buildings, worth about fifteen
thousand dollars. Much of this land lies on the

best streets of the village, and is laid out into lots, averaging about one hundred feet by three hundred, which are held at one hundred dollars a lot. It owns also about twenty-five good business lots, twenty-five feet by one hundred and twenty-five, held at one hundred to one hundred and fifty dollars a lot. The College has an endowment of ninety-five thousand dollars, not including the land. Our debts are about ten thousand dollars. Our current expenses are about ten thousand dollars, and our income seven thousand. The balance is made up by benevolent contributions. Many of our students are admitted free of tuition, on account of funds contributed for that object; hence our income from that source is very small; tuition is only nominal, being but six dollars to nine dollars a year.

DEPARTMENTS OF THE COLLEGE.

The constituency of the College is such as to compel the keeping up of all grades of schools from the primary to the college proper. It is especially a school for the poor, and for those who have had little or no opportunity for education. It keeps up primary, intermediate and grammar schools; and divides the superior portion of the school into classical, literary, normal and preparatory departments, with about the usual courses of study in the several departments. A year of French or German is required in the College course. The literary course is designed not only for ladies, but for gentlemen who desire a thorough English education without Greek, and with only the amount of Latin required for entering college. The normal course is what its name implies. No department of the Institution is of greater importance than this. Kentucky has no greater need than a large reinforcement of competent, native school-teachers, both white and colored. There is no great demand for foreign teachers. The native born will generally be preferred, and they are sufficiently numerous to meet all demands.

STUDENTS.

Our whole number of students since the war has been seventeen hundred and four. Many of them have spent from three to six years here, but few have graduated. The standard of education among the patrons of this school is so low that few can see the propriety of studying six or seven years after having acquired a better education than a majority of their teachers have. Our first college class, which graduated in 1873, consisted of three white young men, all natives of Kentucky. The next class consisted of four young men, two white and two colored. Our whole number of graduates is thirty-six. Two have died, three are farmers or stock-raisers, one has been superintendent of colored emigration to Kansas, one is in business, the others occupy important positions as teachers or preach- ers. A majority of the graduates are white.

Of the whole number of our students two- fifths, as nearly as we can estimate, have become teachers. The annual number of students for the last few years has been about four hundred. In one year they represented fifty-eight towns in Kentucky, and eleven other states.

FACULTY AND INSTRUCTORS.

The whole number of teachers who have been connected with this school from the beginning, not including students who have taught classes occasionally, is forty-nine, nineteen males and thirty females. They have come from ten differ- ent states, and twenty-seven of them were edu- cated at Oberlin College in Ohio.

The present corps of teachers is as follows:

Rev. E. H. Fairchild, President, Professor of Mental and Moral Philosophy.

Rev. John G. Fee, A. M., Lecturer on Evi- dences of Christianity and Biblical Literature.

L. V. Dodge, A. M., Professor of Greek and Acting Professor of Mathematics.

Rev. Walter E. C. Wright, A. M., Professor of Natural Science.

Rev. B. S. Hunting, A. M., Principal of the Preparatory Department and Acting Professor of Latin.

P. D. Dodge, A. B., Instructor in German and Book-Keeping.

Miss Lucia A. Darling, Principal of the Ladies' Department.

Miss Maria A. Muzzy, Assistant Principal.

Miss Kate Gilbert, Instructor in Latin and French.

Miss Jennie E. Lester, A. B., Teacher of Normal Preparatory.

Miss Emma F. More, Teacher of Secondary School.

Miss Ida M. Clark, Teacher of Primary School.

Miss Eurie J. Hamilton, Teacher of Vocal and Instrumental Music.

Miss Anna M. Johnston, Teacher in Preparatory Department.

BOARD OF TRUSTEES.

Rev. J. A. R. Rogers, Shawano, Wis.
Morgan Burdett, Berea.
Elisha Harrison, Berea.
Arthur J. Hanson, Berea.
William Hart, Berea.
Charles Lester, Berea.
Jordon C. Jackson, Lexington.
J. Speed Smith, Richmond.

PRUDENTIAL COMMITTEE.

Rev. E. H. Fairchild, *Chairman.*   Rev. J. G.
Fee; John G. Hanson; Charles Lester; P. D.
Dodge, *Secretary.*
Treasurer and Steward, P. D. Dodge.

LADIES' BOARD OF CARE.

Mrs. Matilda H. Fee, *President*; Mrs. L. M.
Dodge; Mrs. Maria B. Fairchild; Miss L. A.
Darling, *Ex-Officio.*
Mrs. H. S. Woodruff, *Matron.*

ITS CHRISTIAN CHARACTER.

The inquiry is often made: "To what religious denomination does Berea College belong?"
We reply, it belongs to none in particular, but
in general to every Church which has living
faith in the Lord Jesus Christ as the Savior from
sin, and is seeking the salvation of the world

through him. Whatever their peculiar views and practices may be, if this is their faith and work, we are heartily with them. They can not be so far astray in anything that we need to have a controversy with them. We will counsel them as brethren if we think they err, but we will not exclude them from our fellowship, nor be excluded by them if we can avoid it.

Our church is called: "The Church at Berea," which is the common style of the New Testament. It holds all the doctrines on which the great mass of the Protestant churches unite, and tolerates every phase of opinion and practice not inconsistent with true Christian character. In its government all members of the church have a vote.

Its pastor, Rev. J. G. Fee, was originally a Presbyterian. In 1852 he embraced the doctrine of immersion and still adheres to it; but he earnestly insists that every true Christian is entitled to a place in the church, whatever his views may be as to the mode and subjects of baptism. While he conscientiously administers only immersion, he as conscientiously yields to his brethren in the church the privilege of other modes and of infant baptism.

Anti-sectarianism is, and always has been, a fundamental principle of Berea College and

church.   In the days of slavery the church refused to fellowship slaveholders and slaveholding
churches, because it believed they were destitute
of Christian character.

It is to advance pure and undefiled religion
that Berea College exists.   It belongs wholly to
Christ, and seeks to educate all its pupils for his
service.   It has no interest in promoting education to be enlisted against Christianity.   We
have occasion often to mourn our want of success, but we regard it as our first and chief duty
to lead our pupils to the Savior of sinners.   We
have occasion also to rejoice that our labors in
this respect are not in vain.   A large majority of
our adult pupils, we hope, are Christians; and
all but three of our graduates are professors of
religion.

POLITICS.

Berea College not only has a religious, it has
also a political character.   It is political because
it is religious.   The Christianity it teaches does
not permit men to ignore their obligations to
maintain, so far as they have the power, a right-
eous government.   We pray for guidance and
success in politics the same as in education and
religion.   Our political principle is: "Thou
shalt love thy neighbor as thyself."   We are not
partisans.   We would not be blind to the faults,

nor submit to the dictation of any party. We believe in equal civil rights to all citizens; and we stand ready to co-operate with that party through which we can most effectually promote that principle. Which that party has been since the opening of the war we have had no difficulty in deciding.

MISSION OF BEREA COLLEGE.

The work of all Christian colleges is in general the same—to promote education, religion and general civilization; to do this by furnishing Christian teachers, preachers and cultured business men to instruct and lead the people. Any such college, well sustained, is an incalculable blessing to any community.

But some colleges have a peculiar responsibility. In the providence of God, or by some special teaching of his Spirit, some great doctrine, or principle, or reform, seems especially intrusted to their keeping and promotion. If this is not, in some measure, true of Berea College, we are in the dark as to wants of the country.

This College sustains peculiar relations to two classes of people, who constitute two-thirds of the population of the State—the colored people and the mountain people.

THE COLORED PEOPLE

Believe that they owe their freedom to the self-denying labors of such men as Mr. Fee, President Fairchild, Prof. Rogers, and that class of men throughout the country who sustain Berea College. They know we are their friends and that we will not deceive them. They believe in our political principles, and though they find it difficult in their modesty to associate with white people on terms of equality, they believe in the principle, and rejoice to see it wrought out. They have their own church relations and modes of worship, and are attached to them like other people, and will not easily fall in with any ideas or modes that are new to them. Yet we are welcome always to all their religious gatherings, and they rejoice to hear the counsels we have to give. Like all uneducated people, they will very gradually learn to appreciate the importance of education. They will not rush into everything good more than other people. But it was never the privilege of any Christian laborers to work for a more grateful, impressible and confiding people.

God has laid upon Berea College special responsibilities in regard to them. Kentucky was never reckoned as a seceding State, and hence was never reorganized by Congress. No provision

was made for the general education of colored
children till ten years ago, and the provision
then made furnished but about one-fourth as
much money per scholar as white schools received, and the school age of their children was
from six to sixteen instead of from six to twenty,
as of the white children. This state of things
continued till a year ago, when a decision of the
United States Court made it necessary to aban-
don this inequality. There is no public sentiment in this State, or in the South generally,
which demands the same education for colored
people as for white. The prevailing idea or sentiment is, that colored people should take the position of servants; that they are out of their place
when appearing anywhere as the equals of white
people. They need education adapted to their
sphere, just enough to aid them in getting a
living in that humble condition. Everything is
deprecated which tends to lift them out of this
condition. As servants, they are welcome every
where, as equals nowhere. A colored driver and
a colored nurse may ride with the family in the
family carriage, but one not a servant must not.
Colored servants may ride in the ladies' car, but
a colored woman not a servant must not. Colored waiters abound in hotels and restaurants,
but colored guests must not appear. Colored

barbers shave and shampoo the most fastidious white people, but the neatest colored man must not be shaved in the same shop. Colored men are good porters on sleeping cars and palace cars, but must not be admitted as passengers. They are cooks and waiters in the most stylish families, but never sit at their tables. A colored preacher, a graduate of a college and theological seminary, ever so able and cultured, would not be invited to dine with his white brother of the same presbytery, if the call to dinner should come while they were in consultation about matters of the church. Thus at every turn, under all circumstances, in language more emphatic than words, they are informed that they are "niggers," and not the equals of white people.

This state of feeling and course of action are prejudicial to them in all their civic and social relations. The negro appears at a disadvantage everywhere. In political conventions and ecclesiastical associations, in arbitrations and suits at law, in educational privileges and business operations, in traveling and in opportunities for social culture, simply because he is a negro he suffers damage.

This must not continue. White and colored people must be perfectly equal before the law. They must have the same civil rights, and be protected alike in the enjoyment of them. We can have no permanent peace, nor, what is more important, any exalted sense of honor and virtue, till this is effectually secured; and it never can be secured till the race prejudice, the caste feeling, the spirit of domination is eradicated.

These distinctions are kept up, not because colored people are personally disagreeable to the white people. There is little such feeling at the South. Not because of their immorality; for as servants they are admitted everywhere. It is simply a caste feeling, a prejudice of position. This feeling controls legislation, it blinds judges and juries, it corrupts executive officers, it biases witnesses. Against this prejudice, or feeling, or taste, or caste, whatever it may be called, Berea College has thoroughly committed itself, and fulfills one of its most important missions in mitigating and removing it.

This it seeks to do through its students, who carry the principles and feelings here imbibed to all parts of the country; by the constant exhibition of perfect equality and perfect harmony to all visitors, and especially to thousands at our annual commencements; by lectures, addresses and sermons of professors and advanced students, to colored, and white, and mixed audiences, gathered for religious, political, or educational purposes; and through the medium of the press. What these influences are accomplishing let a beholder and not an actor answer. Prof. A. P. Peabody, of Harvard, closes a very able article in the *Unitarian Review*, on the Co-education of the Races, with the following paragraph :—

Of all the experiments in co-education that have been instituted, we regard Berea College, in Kentucky, as the most important in its sphere of influence and in its prophecy of enduring benefit to the colored race. It has carried the war into the enemy's camp, and has brought its whole Christian panoply and armament into the immediate encounter with the surviving spirit of slavery—a spirit made all the more virulent by the destruction of its body. At other institutions black students are admitted to an equality with the white; at Berea white students are admitted to an equality with the black.* The trustees and professors at Berea can not invite their white neighbors to unite with them in throwing the doors of their Institution wide open to all that choose to come. They must first gather their little flock of black pupils, with a very few white youths from their own or friendly families, and then they must make their light shine bright enough and far enough to win the regard and confidence of a distrustful and scornful public, and to demonstrate to that unwilling public that it is for their own and their children's interest that they patronize this Institution. This has been effected. The

---

* NOTE. A slight mistake as to the origin of the school.

College has shown its large educational capacity. Its public exercises have been attended in successive years by persons of established reputation as educationists and literary men, and have received their unqualified commendation and praise. There is, for many miles around, no institution of learning that does nearly so much or so well for its pupils. The consequence is that those at first vehemently opposed to it are fast falling into the ranks of neutrals or friends. Many who deemed it a nuisance have already sent their children to it. Its sterling value as a seminary of education is now recognized on all hands. But it is of much more worth for its si lent, yet most efficient, propagandism of the due relation between the races; for co-education includes within itself, or involves as its necessary consequence, equality in all civic and social rights, immunities, duties and obligations.

Moreover, a State in which white citizens already seek for their children the privilege of co-education with colored youths, can not long retain its hostility to public schools common to both races. The universal establishment of such schools in the late slave States is, as we have said, essential to their political and social well-being; and for the advancement of this end Berea College is now doing more than can be effected by any possible legislation, by any action of political parties, or by the combined influence of press, platform and pulpit.

For two principal reasons we advocate the co-education of the races. 1. It is impossible to educate both races separately. In the rural dis-

6

tricts it is impossible, in most cases, to maintain
two sets of schools.   In the cities it may be
done, but in the country it can not.   In hundreds of districts there are very few, from five
to twenty-five, colored children.   They must be
admitted to the schools which white children
attend, or be left without schools.   In other dis-
tricts the same is true of white children.   In
some counties there are barely colored children
enough for a single school.   2. The separation
fosters a spirit of contempt, and haughtiness,
and domineering on the one side, and a sense of
debasement, and a spirit of sycophancy or surli-
ness on the other, entirely inconsistent with the
highest good of either.   It is cruel and abusive
to teach the colored children from the very beginning that they are only fit for servants of
white people, and are not at all to be tolerated
in the same school-room with white children.
Such treatment will never make them self-re-
specting, patriotic, independent citizens.

There is nothing, in the absence of co-education, which can secure the mutual regard, confidence and honorable deportment which must
exist between these races, if we are to have a
peaceful, intelligent and virtuous community.

We are well aware that in seeking to work
such a revolution in Southern society, we accept

a herculean task. We are not greeted with cheers and applause at every step. We have learned to get on without them. We know that God approves, and that many true friends pray for us, and are ready to share the burden. We also know that our cause will triumph. We have seen much greater revolutions both at the North and the South. Fifty years ago the whole nation was agitated when a single college admitted colored students. Now very few colleges at the North reject them. In common schools the change is hardly less. The South will change more rapidly, for there is little color prejudice to be overcome. If the laws of the State prohibiting co-education were repealed, many districts would at once admit the few colored children they have.

THE MOUNTAIN PEOPLE.

When we speak of this class of people at the North, we soon hear the words: "Poor white trash!" We wish to say at the outset that they sustain no relation to that miserable class of people. The "poor white trash" have sustained a miserable existence, by petty jobs and petty pilfering among slaveholders, and were despised by the slaves themselves. Kentucky has had but a small share of them. But wherever they are we must not despise them. They are victims of a great wrong, and need our help. The mountain people have been almost entirely separated from slavery and slaveholders, and have had little interest in them; and have been, in the main, independent of them. Had Kentucky been wholly a slaveholding State, it would have been wholly a rebel State. But it was neutral; not because its individual men were neutral, but because its zealous rebel element was neutralized by a union element just as zealous. The mountain men were nearly all for the union, and some counties furnished more union soldiers than they had men liable to military duty. A few mountain men were violent rebels, and a few slaveholders were ready to sacrifice everything for the union. But the grand division was between the mountains and the plains; and there is the same division still. The mountain counties are generally republican, some of them almost exclusively so; and the Blue Grass counties are democratic, their white population almost entirely so. Thus, though the mountain people were not abolitionists, and had no special sympathy with the colored people as slaves, there are now several bonds of union between them. They agree in politics, and are working together to overthrow the aristocratic rebel party; and

they are destined to succeed. They are much
alike in their style of living. Being generally
poor, they are obliged to work for their daily
bread, and enjoy but few of the luxuries of life,
and look with the same sort of jealousy upon
the aristocracy. They have alike been deprived
of the advantages of education. One-fourth of
the adult population of the mountains can not
read. The rich have had little more interest in
general education than in the education of their
slaves, and the neglect is felt by them in some
measure alike. They feel that they are looked
upon with about the same haughty contempt by
many of the aristocracy, and in this respect they
have a fellow-feeling.

It is from the mountain people that the most
of our white students come. It is generally a
great trial to them to think of associating with
colored people. They have their prejudices to
overcome. But they find it easier to endure it
than to endure the manners of aristocratic students. And the expenses of schools for the
wealthy are entirely beyond their reach. Probably no school out of the mountains has so large
a representation from them as this. Nothing
but poverty prevents their coming in large numbers. It would be easy to crowd our buildings

to overflowing, if we could assure them that they could pay their expenses by manual labor.

To this people we have access. We are invited to their Sunday-school conventions and teachers' institutes; and their churches are open to us when we choose to occupy them. They seek our aid in establishing Sunday-schools, and our students teach many of their day schools. They thankfully receive second-hand libraries furnished through us by Northern churches and Sunday-schools. About twenty Sunday-schools were organized in a single year through the influence of these libraries. It is a very simple way of accomplishing much good.

As the State common-school system improves, these mountain people will improve, and their political power will increase. There are among them men of property, and education, and moral power; and such men sometimes come from fifty to a hundred miles on horseback to attend our commencements, and carry back reports of what they have seen. Often they come with their prejudices and return without them, or greatly modified.

There is not a more needy or important field of labor than these mountains, and the only limit to the labor we can perform in it is the limit of our numbers, time and strength. The majority of the people live in log houses, and very many of them in houses without glass windows. Their school-houses very often have no windows, and often no doors, and sometimes no floors. In traveling through six counties the writer saw but one painted and plastered school-house. Where they have churches they usually have preaching about once a month, and their preach- ers receive little or no compensation. They are commonly laboring men; and nothing is more common than to hear them assure their hearers that they are not indebted to their "book-learn- ing," but to the Spirit for their sermons. These people are not to be suddenly transformed to an intelligent, industrious, cultured people. Very many of their schools are taught but three months in the year, with few books, no maps, and no blackboards, and by teachers poorly qualified to give oral instruction. They gener- ally have no libraries and take no papers. Those who are able to read, read but very little. Frequently but one paper, and sometimes not one, is taken in a school district. The most hopeful means of doing them good is to induce many of their most promising young men and women to go to some good school and fit them- selves for teachers

This is the field of Berea College. We have

had students from twelve different States at a
time, but our great work is among the poor people of Kentucky. Young men have walked
sixty miles to get here, and sometimes without
a dollar, hoping here to find work to pay their
way. Two young men came sixty-five miles
with a pair of two-year-old calves before a cart
to haul their baggage, and a boy to drive the
team back.

A mountain girl was so impressed at commencement that she told her mother she must
go to school. She said if she had five hundred
dollars she would give it all to be able to read
such essays as some of those young ladies read.
Her parents had no money, and depended on
her to make their "crap." But she found a
place to work for her board, and in emergencies
went home to help about the crop, and with
great perseverance and determination she was
enabled in two years to teach school; and a year
after, though her studies were by no means complete, the *Mountain Echo*, in giving an account
of a teachers' institute, reported her as having
read two essays, for which she received votes of
thanks; and made a statement as to her mode of
managing a school, which was highly compli-
mented. We must not multiply individual

cases, interesting as they are to us. "The poor have the gospel preached to them."

The mission of Berea College also embraces efforts, through its professors, to promote Christian union and vital piety. A State association has been organized, called: "The State Association of Christian Ministers and Churches of Kentucky," and looks after the interests of feeble churches, and seeks to supply destitute places. The association is small, but we hope not useless.

Our great desire is to aid in elevating the standard of holy living; to promote Christian activity, through Sunday-schools and prayer-meetings; to encourage family prayer and more regard for the Sabbath; to promote temperance and abstinence from deadly weapons. Two of the greatest evils of Kentucky are whisky and pistols. Yet there is considerable interest on the subject of temperance, and many voting dis-tricts (we have no townships) have voted no license, according to the provisions of the local option law. The Glade District, in which Berea is, voted no license, by a majority of four to one. Many drinking men voted no license.

The religion of the South is such as might naturally be expected to accompany the system of slavery. Christians who practiced and defended

7

slave-holding should not be expected to have very exalted ideas of love to God and man. They probably feel the need of religion as much as any people, and contrive to have it in some form; yet it would not be strange if they should shrink from bringing their lives very near to God in the prayer: "Search me, O God, and know my heart, and see if there be any evil way in me." There seems to be much lack of prayer. Family worship is the exception, and by no means the rule in Christian families. A prominent Presbyterian preacher, well known in Kentucky, had been spending a Sabbath in a village of two thousand inhabitants, where churches are abundant, and the elder, by whom he was entertained, expressed the belief that his family was the only one in the town which kept up a family altar. This was probably a mistake; yet it is the belief of intelligent preachers, who have traveled extensively in the State, that few Christian families maintain family worship.

THE KU-KLUX

Never paid us a visit. Many rumors of their hostile intentions reached us, and rumors that our College buildings and some of our private houses had been burned, spread through the country; but, from what we knew of their operations near us, we did not apprehend any disturbance from them. For a year or two, about 1870 and later, the country was completely under their control. There was no protection for anybody against whom their violence was directed. One night they took possession of Richmond, to the number, as was said, of a hundred and fifty or more, took a man from the jail, who had given himself up to the authorities and was awaiting trial, and hung him in the Court House yard; and pinned an order upon his back, directing that he should hang there till four P. M. the next day; and there he hung, in a village of fifteen hundred inhabitants, where hundreds were passing every hour, till the time appointed, no authority venturing to interfere. It was said that the man was a desperado, and had killed several persons, and deserved to be hung. It may have been so, but it is claimed by others that he had acted in self-defense. The best place to ascertain those facts and correct them was in the Court House, by the appointed authorities, and not at midnight, by a band of lawless ruffians.

One night they took two negroes from the jail, whipped one and hung the other, and ordered that he should hang till eleven A. M., and then be buried on a certain farm near Silver Creek, and the order was obeyed.

They hung a man one Saturday night within three miles of Berea. It was rumored that he had participated in a murder during the war, but there was never an investigation.

To record all the accounts that have reached us of their lawless violence would fill a large book· Their object was not robbery, as some have supposed; nor, in this region, did it seem to be political; nor was their attention directed especially against the colored people. They had old grudges to avenge, and new misdemeanors to regulate; and it appeared as if many prominent men preferred that method of keeping things in order. The negroes were constantly in alarm, and white Republicans nearly as much so, for it was understood that neither of those parties was represented in the bands.

These organizations seem to have disbanded years ago, soon after a large number of them had been arrested by United States authority. Much opposition was made to this interference of the General Government, as was to be expected; but the General Government never performed a more humane or timely deed. The whole State was under the control of the Ku-Klux for years, very many murders were committed, and innumerable deeds of violence; yet if a single member of the Klan was ever punished by the State authorities, it has not come to our knowledge. This is not to be charged altogether to the indifference or collusion of State officers. If they had been ever so much disposed to punish them, it would have been very difficult. They were so numerous and had so many sympathizers that justice was impossible. All this has passed away.

ANNOYANCES.

Those very common annoyances of tramps and burglars we have been exempt from; being too poor to present a temptation, or too remote from the railroad for their convenience. Our beggars we soon become acquainted with, and have seldom a new case to investigate.·

The most serious annoyance of Berea is the riding through the streets of intoxicated men, shouting and occasionally firing their pistols, not careful where the balls may strike. This has greatly diminished, and is chiefly confined to seasons of exciting elections, and to persons from abroad.

The disposition to injure Berea seems to have passed away. For several years the inhabitants have felt as safe as the inhabitants of most Northern villages. If we have more armed rowdies, we have less robbers and burglars.

It is exceedingly wonderful, and according to human calculations unaccountable, that during all these years of opposition to Berea and her people, no one has received injury to his person. Any good people, who would like a pleasant Southern home, with unlimited opportunities for usefulness and superior educational advantages, would be foolish to avoid Berea from fear of violence.

OSTRACISM.

It has been the common lot of most teachers of colored schools, and, to some extent, of business men from the North, to be isolated and deprived of all, or nearly all white society. It is not so here. While many people undoubtedly have no desire to cultivate our acquaintance, we have right about us more white Kentucky friends of excellent character, who invite us to their houses, than we have time to visit as we desire. Some of the principal families in Richmond exchange visits with us, and some in Lexington, and some in Louisville, and so in many places through the Blue Grass region we are welcome, and almost everywhere in the mountains.

Our business relations with Kentucky people are as agreeable as could be desired. Our patronage is sought, and credit is offered us to suit our convenience. Banks accommodate us cheerfully and bountifully, with no other security than our signatures. Of course we pay, or our credit would fail. We have no reason to think that our credit is in the least affected by the fact that most of us are Northern men.

The reputation of the College as a school is also good. It is perfectly common to hear it called the best school in the State. Of course all such compliments are received with much allowance for carelessness of language, and want of information in regard to the schools of the State. But though as compliments such expressions will hardly bear criticism, as indications of feeling they are significant.

REGULATIONS.

A little book of rules is given to every student on entering the school. It is unnecessary to give quotations from these rules, but a few general statements may be desirable.

Applicants for admission to the school must bring certificates of good moral character, and students must maintain such a character, not only while in school, but during their absence in vacation. They are required to abstain entirely from the use of intoxicating drinks, and are not allowed to use tobacco in or about the College buildings or premises, or in other public places.

They are advised to give up tobacco entirely, and the most of them do. They are not allowed to keep fire-arms in their rooms, nor to use them in any way without permission. They are also prohibited from frequenting places of public resort, or absenting themselves from any school duties, or leaving town without permission; and young men are required to be in their own rooms after ten o'clock at night, and young ladies after half past seven, during the fall and winter, and eight during the spring term.

No secret societies are allowed in the Institution, and students are not allowed to have any active connection with such societies while in attendance at the school.

The religious exercises upon which students are required to attend are one preaching service and a Bible class upon the Sabbath, a religious lecture or sermon on Tuesday, and a Bible class on Thursday, and daily prayers, in the morning at the chapel. At all these exercises there is almost perfect punctuality, and there are no indications that they are felt to be burdensome.

The uniting of the two sexes in the same school is an innovation in Kentucky, and the regulations pertaining to their social intercourse are among the most important. They recite in the same classes when pursuing the same studies, and attend the same religious exercises and scientific lecturers, but do not belong to the same literary societies, nor do they visit each other's societies except on public occasions. They must not attend each other to and from religious meetings; but may, with special permission, at the regular monthly scientific lectures, and other occasional public literary exercises. They take their meals in the same dining hall and at the same tables, but room in separate buildings, about sixty rods apart, and concealed from each other by a grove of forest trees. They must never call at each other's rooms, except by special permission in case of sickness, on pain of expulsion. Young men, at certain designated hours, may, with special permission, meet young ladies at the public parlors; general social gatherings are occasionally permitted; and sometimes parties are allowed, with proper supervision, to ride to the mountains; but single couples are never permitted to ride or walk by themselves. It is our conviction, after much experience and much investigation, that in a well-managed school such a union of the sexes as is here described is profitable to both parties, and adds much to the interest and refining influences of all social and religious meetings. The young men have prayer-meetings by themselves, as do the ladies also, and they have a weekly young people's prayer-meeting in which both unite. The *a priori* theories, which many hold in opposition to the co education of the sexes, are generally dispelled by a little of the proper kind of experience.

EXPENSES.

It is the desire of the Trustees to bring the advantages of the school, as far as possible, within the reach of all. The charges for room rent, fuel and incidentals, are barely sufficient to pay expenses and keep the buildings in repair. The highest tuition is nine dollars a year, and provision has been made for free tuition to a large number of the needy. Instrumental music is seven dollars for twelve lessons, with use of instrument daily for three months. Vocal music is free. Board is six dollars a month; barely sufficient, with a large number of boarders, to pay the cost. A student is furnished with board, a furnished room, fuel, lights and tuition for seventy-five dollars a year. This must be paid quarterly in advance. When paid monthly in advance the expense is a trifle more.

In thus reducing expenses we have not been unmindful of the truth that that which costs nothing is generally esteemed to be worth nothing. The price of board alone at the lowest possible rate is entirely beyond the reach of the most of those who would be glad to patronize this school. Seventy-five dollars a year to the average of our patrons is more than a thousand dollars to the average of those who send their sons and daughters through college. We find it necessary not only to make expenses as low as possible, but to furnish all possible opportunities for students to defray a portion of their expenses by means of manual labor. Some defray half, and some more than half, in this way. Contributions to enable promising youth to attend the school, who would otherwise be unable, have been most gratefully received.

DONORS.

There is a class of men, and women too, of whom we can not speak as we feel, without offense to them. We are grateful to them every day and cherish their names in our hearts, and feel like giving them here. But they do not sound a trumpet before them when they give alms, nor do they wish others to do it for them. They are our fellow-workers in this labor of love, no less essential to it than those on the ground; and evince equal faith and interest in it as the work of God. Their motives are not appreciated by a portion of the Southern people. A South

Carolina editor, after having been kindly entertained and led through the principal buildings,
and shown all that he wished to see, gave, in his
paper, a full and flattering account of the school
and the buildings, expressing his opposition, of
course, to the co-education of the races, and then
pronounced the whole "the work of Northern
spite." We hope that he, and some others like
him, may live to appreciate a class of men whose
all-controlling motives are entirely above their
conception. Many good men in the South regard
it as a work of real but mistaken benevolence.
A few look upon it as a wonderful work of God,
and the number of such is constantly increasing.
A few only have sufficiently identified themselves with the work to feel it a privilege to
contribute to it. A few thousand dollars only
have been received from Kentucky. We prize
one thousand from Kentuckians more than two
from other sources, and we shall not fail to furnish them the opportunity very often, to share
in this good work.

To the honor of Christianity, and for the encouragement of those who may follow us, we
wish to bear testimony that our efforts in raising
money have brought us into contact with many
such glorious, warm-hearted men of wealth as
we did not suppose the world contained. While

we have met numerous striking illustrations of
the saying, "It is easier for a camel to go
through a needle's eye than for a rich man to
enter the kingdom of heaven," we have found
not a few rich men to whom the gates are wide
open. They have "made to themselves friends
of the mammon of unrighteousness, who shall
receive them to everlasting habitations."

PRESENT WANTS.

Our first want is ten thousand dollars to pay
our debts. We want ten thousand dollars to
build a Recitation Hall, which is very much
needed. We want three thousand dollars for
the current expenses of the ensuing year. If
then fifty thousand dollars could be added to
our endowment, our pecuniary wants would be
met, probably for ten years.

Another want of Berea is good Christian inhabitants to surround the school with an atmosphere of intelligence and Christian love. If
there is any place where a life of energy, purity,
meekness, love, faith and patience will redound
to the glory of God and the salvation of men, it
is here. Farmers, mechanics, fruit-growers,
dairy-men, if you desire to find a mild climate
and a pleasant home, but especially to do good,
come and see us.

Our last, and first, and greatest want, compared with which all others dwindle to insignificance, is the blessing of God. Without this we want nothing else, we ask nothing, we can do nothing, we can hope for nothing. If He had not been on our side in many dangers and straits, we should have failed. If He go not with us still, we shall still fail. Reader, please pray for us.

AMERICAN MISSIONARY ASSOCIATION.

We can not, without injustice to ourselves and friends, close this narrative without paying our tribute of gratitude to that association, which, almost from the beginning of Mr. Fee's labors in the State, has given its constant support to this work. Though it never exercised any control over Berea College, and can not, with propriety, be said to have founded it; yet, but for its pecuniary aid, and its perennial stream of encouragement, counsel, sympathy and cheer in all the days and years of darkness, danger, doubt and fear, who can say that the College would ever have existed? or that this mission could have been continued?

This association was in this field with the gospel of freedom when all other organizations working here succumbed to slavery; it met the first contrabands with schools and the gospel at the opening of the war; and it has been the principal agency by which the Southern work, the most important of this generation, has been carried on to the present time. We wish its patronage were multiplied many fold. Our esteem and reverence for that society partake much of the affection of children for parents, yet we believe we can speak of its work with intelligent impartiality.

Continuation

OUR READERS will be interested to learn something of the years which have passed since this little volume was written. They have been years of change, of progress, and Berea stands at the threshhold of a new era—an enlarged mission.

We can here record only a few leading events.

VISIT OF GEO. W. CABLE.

The Commencement of 1885 was signalized by the visit of several distinguished christian gentlemen, including Judge Beckner of Winchester, Mr. Robert West of Chicago, and Dr. Washington Gladden of Columbus. The most notable feature of the occasion was the address of Geo. W. Cable in which Berea was styled "A College which forecasts the Millenium."

ROSWELL C. SMITH.

About this time Mr. Roswell C. Smith of the Century Company became interested in Berea, and employed an agent to travel through Kentucky, ostensibly for business purposes, but really to gather opinions regarding the work of this school. Mr. Smith became convinced that Berea was in a position to perform an unparalleled service to the

country in opposing the spirit of caste and effacing
sectional lines.   He entered upon the work of
building up the college with great earnestness,
writing many personal letters in its behalf, and
meeting nearly the entire expense of a new recitation building named at his request Lincoln Hall.

LINCOLN HALL.

Mr. Smith's illness and death cut short this noble
work, but the superb building stands as a monu-
ment to his wise beneficence, and a lasting addition to the equipment of the College.

PRESIDENT FROST.

Professor Wm. G. Frost of Oberlin had been selected by Brother Fee and President Fairchild to
be the latter's successor, and he was elected at the
Trustee meeting in 1888.   For family reasons
Prof. Frost declined this call.   President Fairchild passed to his reward soon after, and for two

years the presidential office was held by Dr. Wm.
B. Stewart, now of Toronto, Canada. On his res-
ignation in 1892 Prof. Frost was a second time
called to the Presidency. He was at the time in
Europe with his family, and upon his return visited Berea and accepted the work.

Rev. Wm. Goodell Frost, D. D., Ph. D., was
born in Le Roy, New York, in 1854, and had already made his mark in several directions.

He is remembered at Oberlin College as a self-
supporting student—though coming from a family
which had enjoyed the privileges of education for
many generations—and as a teacher of great vig-
or and popularity. He is known to a wider
circle as the author of a remarkably progressive
"Greek Primer," "Inductive Studies in Oratory,"
and other scholarly works.

Although never holding pastoral charge, he is
an earnest and effective preacher. He has been
identified with the work of the Ohio State Y. M.
C. A., and for many years was leader of a young
people's prayer meeting attended by above four
hundred students.

President Frost has raised considerable sums of
money for Oberlin College, won some repute as a
lyceum lecturer, and even made a brief but brill-
iant excursion into politics.

Graduating at Oberlin in 1876, and pursuing
post-graduate courses at Wooster University, Harvard, Andover, and abroad, he has made a lifelong
study of educational methods and visited the leading institutions of both Europe and America.

And he has been providentially prepared by his
Puritan ancestry, Oberlin training, and connection
with public life, for the peculiar work of Berea.

DR. LEAVITT IN THE NEW YORK *Independent.*

President Frost has some unusual adaptations for the work in Berea, quite apart from his proficiency as a teacher and his accom-
plishments as a scholar. He is a reformer. He is an orator. He
is an evangelist. He is a politician of the high type of Garfield
He is an enthusiast. He is a born leader. With a proper suppo,
from the donors old and new, the following things may be expect
ed for Berea under the administration of President Frost: Students will be drawn to it from both sides of the Ohio River. Its
three hundred and fifty students will soon be five hundred, and
then a thousand. The present departments will be re-inforced.
New departments will be opened. * *

THE NEW BEREA.

President Frost was scarcely on the ground
when the financial storm broke over the country.
Despite the storm, however, Berea has been providentially sustained, and its work reorganized and
enlarged. The number of students has increased
in one year nearly forty per cent. Special features
in the new administration have been:

1. Improved courses and methods of instruction which have enabled Berea to offer

"Northern Advantages in Southern Mountain Climate"

and thus draw students from a dozen northern
states.

This is a grand thing in many ways. It brings
College students into contact with missionary
work. It increases the body of Christian workers
who coöperate with the Faculty and teachers. It
introduces to each other representative young
people of the north and the south.

To many it offers educational opportunities otherwise quite unattainable. Between Park College in Missouri and the Moody schools in Massachusetts there is no christian institution where the expenses are so moderate. *The outlay for board and all college expenses for a school year is less than $100.* This enables one to live *comfortably.* Whatever the student earns can be applied to diminishing this small outlay. These low expenses are due to most careful management, and still more to an unrivalled location.

If this were Perea's only mission it would be enough—to gather those who would otherwise despair of an education, and train them in science, literature, and applied Christianity together!

2. A newly organized Normal Course, under the College management, which will give the Institution a leavening influence through the public schools which are now being developed in the South.

3. Domestic Industry and Manual Training. In spite of the hard times means have been secured for a "Model House" designed to show what the home of a family of limited means should be, and affording a place for instruction in sewing, cooking, etc. Miss Adelia Fox of Toledo has come as a volunteer worker in this department, and is a lady of rare qualifications for the position.

A fine new building is also provided for Manual Training, containing dressing room, power room, iron room, wood room, draughting room, and printing room—erected by student labor.

We have thus a pecularly perfect form of "College Settlement." Pres. Frost said in his Inaugural, "The methods of instruction in elementary, manual, and collegiate work should be differant, and we claim that they are more certain to be different when carried on under one intelligent management. * * Berea College stands with a spade and a spelling book in one hand, and a telescope and a Greek Testament in the other."

REV. A. D. MAYO ON THE NEW SOUTH.

The progress of the South has reached a point of great interest, and the work of Berea during the next two decades will be of the utmost importance. The situation is thus sketched by one who has the highest right to speak with authority:*

"The preliminary struggle is over, the "mixed," educational feature, at Berea, being an accepted fact; and the great coming interest of the institution is now converging on the most vital problem of southern education for the coming generation, —the training of the Southern "third estate," the masses of the white people who were never slaveholders, in the education required for the American citizenship of to day.

LATEST PHASE OF THE SOUTHERN PROBLEM—RISE OF "THE CRACKERS."

Our New England people do not realize as they should that this is the present "solid South," of

*[Dr. Mayo has devoted the past sixteen years to a special study of education in the South, visiting every southern state repeatedly, and preparing reports for the U. S. Government. This article was prepared after his third visit to Berea, without consultation with any officer of the College, and gives the unbiased judgment of one of the few men best qualified to estimate the providential opening now before Berea.]

which they hear so much and know so little. In three-forths of the old slave States to-day the political power has forever departed from the old-time slave-holding aristocracy that brought on the war. Under the name "Farmers' Alliance," "Populist," or with no special name, by the capture of 'he regular political machine, including the shrewdest of the professional politicians, the vhite masses, whom we met thirty years ago as he almost invincible Confederate soldiery, now confront us, through their representatives in Washington, demanding what amounts to a revolution more radical and far-reaching in the industrial and financial policy of the republic than that against which the entire North revolted under the leadership of Abraham Lincoln in 1860. Not only the destiny of the Negro, but the prosperity of the South and of the whole country, is involved in the fit educational training of this vast coming New South. *

The Southern Negro to-day is a man at the bottom of a deep ditch. Treading on him is the white man of the class now come in power, and at the top what remains of the Southern "aristocracy" of half a century ago. We cannot extricate the Negro without lifting the others! And the uneducated white man is the most difficult to deal with. Up to the present time about everything done for the Negro by the Southern people has been the work of the old master class, who constituted till 1860 the educated upper strata of these States. It is through their influence that the common school and the opportunity for industrial uplift has been mainly achieved. To-day, under the administration of the white non-slaveholding people of the South, *there is more danger of an arrest of progress for the seven million colored folk than for the past twenty years.* A whole generation of common-school educat'on in the open country, with all that belongs thereto, is the great hope of Southern civilization for the near future.

THE MOST FAVORABLE POINT.

In cne sense, the two or three millions of white people who occupy this vast Appalachian region of the Central South and the intermediate rim that separates it from the lowlands is the most favorable point of approach for philanthropic effort in this great work. These people were almost unanimous in their devotion to the Union in the War; and, whenever reached by our armies, they enlisted, forming of themselves a great army of a hundred and fifty thousand men that followed the old flag. Their country today has a greater outcome in the near future than any region east of the Mississippi.

BEREA IS THE LEVER.

Just on the border of this great educational mission field now stands Berea College, by all odds with better equipment. more valuable experience, and larger opportunities for doing this work than any school with which I am acquainted. In religion, as in race, it is "no respector of persons." Its colony of Northern students is a great addition to the value of the school, and quite without a parallel in institutions of the kind. Its teaching force is superior to that of any school in the South supported by the north; while, in itself, it is a native growth, from the stern necessities of the progressive life of one of the foremost Southern States. It is now on the eve of important reorganization, especially in the direction of training teachers for the mountain country and putting on the ground a thorough scheme of industrial training.

A WORK WE ALL BELIEVE IN.

In my ministry of education I do not "bate a jot of heart or hope" for the blessed work of educating the Negro. Hampton and Tuskegee and Atlanta and other schools for the race are firmly established in the heart of northern philanthropy. But none of them is more deserving to be placed in the same rank, as one of the permanent objects of future generous giving from New England, than Berea. There is no Southern people more in need of educational training for good citizenship, none which responds more eagerly to opportunity, than the great constituency of Berea College. With the fit means in hand, in five years Berea might easily have an attendance from this source alone as numerous as Harvard University, with such an opportunity for the highest usefulness as exists nowhere beyond the shadow of this glorious Appalachian upland realm.

In this wonderful region is to be the theater of the next great campaign of Universal Education in this country. In no part of the Union is there, to-day, such a call for a great revival of everything called education as in this region. But of all the schools that have undertaken to grapple with the mighty problem of lifting up this immense region to the higher civilization, none is so favorably situated, or today in so good condition to accomplish a great work, as Berea college. Probably no where in the United States would an endowment of a million dollars do more for the great cause of Universal Education than right here."

THE NEEDS OF THE WORK.   HOW ALL MAY HELP.

Berea must have 250 "sustaining scholarships," of $40. each, or their equivalent, annually provided by those who believe in this work.

It must have 50 "working scholarships" of $40. each,—the money to be paid for work in the printing office, boarding hall, etc., *doing good twice*, relieving the Institution of expense, and aiding needy and promising students while cultivating a spirit of self-reliance.

It must have 25 "gift scholarships" of $75 each for special cases—students whose need and promise of usefullness are well ascertained. Many of these will be divided between several students.

Berea is in need of permanent endowment.

Money orders should be made payable to the Treasurer of Berea College.

Bequests should be made to the Board of Trustees of Berea College, Berea, Madison Co., Ky.

The following paper is a summary of the aims and mission of Berea College, and must be an effective call for large coöperation on the part of all who pray for the coming kingdom:

A Call.

The peculiar work and opportunity of Berea College place it quite apart from all other institutions, and give it a special claim upon the attention of every Christian and patriot.

Situated near the center of population, and furnishing an education of the best type—industrial, normal, collegiate—to multitudes who would otherwise fail of such advantages, it exerts a potent influence in favor of progressive and Christian ideas.

But *beyond this*, having been founded among anti-slavery Kentuckians before the war, and having shown a courage that compels respect, Berea is in a position to do an unparalled service to the country in opposing the spirit of caste and effacing sectional lines.

Berea is distinctively Christian, but controlled by no sect, and there is no denominational school which has before it this providential opening.

Until larger endowments can be secured, about $12,000 must be provided each year by contributions from friends of the cause.

We not only seek the large benefactions of the rich, but earnestly invite every one who approves of this work to contribute, according to his ability, any sum from $5.00 to $5,000.

Each signer of this appeal is a personal contributor.

Geo. W. Cable,   Herrick Johnson,

    Hiram C. Hayden,   Fredrick Douglass,

      Geo. R. Leavitt,   Josiah Strong,

Chas. G. Ames,   Albert Shaw,

    Cassius M. Clay,   A. D. Mayo,

     Geo. W. Julian, and many others.

No better guarantee of the stability and wise administration of the Institution can be given than the names of its present board of Trustees.

TRUSTEES.

Catalogue giving latest information mailed to any address on application to the President or Secretary.